Dear Parents,

Every day we measure time or distance, look for patterns, estimate, and count. Whether we realize it or not, we are constantly thinking mathematically.

Children are given a great deal of encouragement when they are learning to count—but the support needn't stop there. Young children love puzzles and riddles, and they eagerly approach problem-solving situations as if they were games. They often see and use a variety of strategies. These are important skills in developing mathematical thinking.

We truly have the power to nurture in our children a long-lasting love for math. We can do this by making a "math connection" to familiar experiences and by supporting our children's natural affinity for the discipline. **Step Into Reading Plus Math** books can help. Each book combines an age-appropriate math element with an enjoyable reading experience.

Remember—math is not an isolated phenomenon but is woven into the fabric of our lives. The love of math is a lifelong journey. Celebrate that journey with your child!

Sincerely,

Colleen DeFoyd

Colleen DeFoyd
Primary Grades Math Teacher
Scottsdale, Arizona

To my dad
—J.G.

For my parents
—R.N.W.

 Published in the United States by Random House, Inc., New York, and simultaneously in Canada by Random House of Canada Limited, Toronto.

http://www.randomhouse.com/

Library of Congress Cataloging-in-Publication Data
Glass, Julie. The fly on the ceiling / by Julie Glass ; illustrated by Richard Walz.
p. cm. – (Step into reading + math)
SUMMARY: A story about how the very messy French philosopher René Descartes invented an ingenious way to keep track of his possessions.
ISBN 0-679-88607-9 (pbk.) — ISBN 0-679-98607-3 (lib. bdg.)
1. Descartes, René, 1596-1650—Juvenile Fiction.
[1. Descartes, René, 1596-1650—Fiction. 2. Graphic methods—Fiction.
3. Orderliness—Fiction.] I. Walz, Richard, ill. II. Title. III. Series.
PZ7.G481235Fl 1998 [E]—dc21 96-6598

Printed in the United States of America 10 9 8 7 6 5

Step into Reading® +Math

The Fly on the Ceiling

A Math Myth

By Dr. Julie Glass
Illustrated by Richard Walz

A Step 3 Book

Random House New York

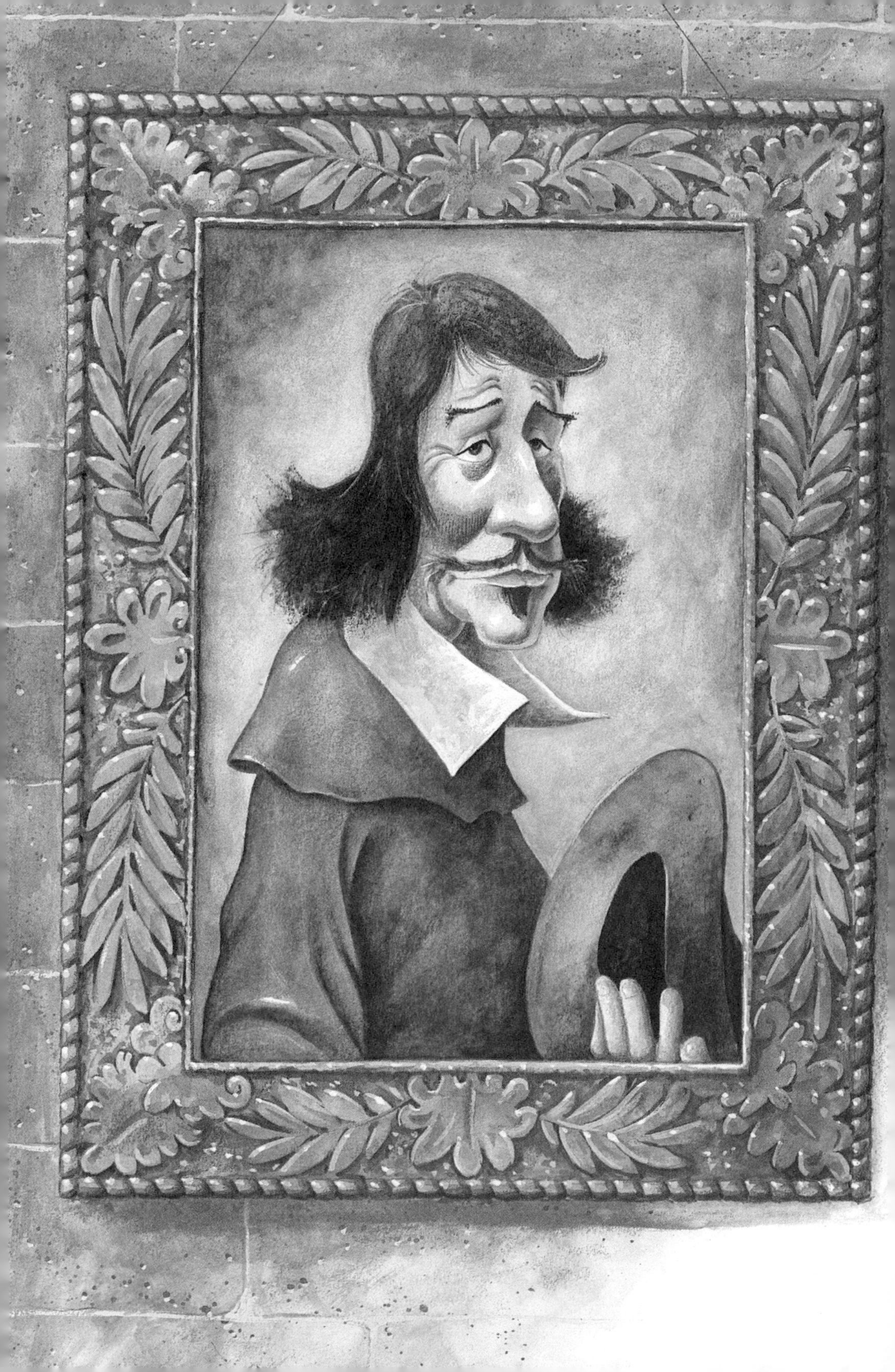

This is the story of a guy who lived a long time ago. He lived in France.

He was a French guy, so he had a French name. His name was René Descartes (pronounced ruh-NAY day-CART). This may sound like a funny name to you, but in France it is perfectly normal.

René was a philosopher. A philosopher is someone who thinks about why things are the way they are.

René was a *great* philosopher. Many of his ideas are still famous today.

But even though René was a great philosopher, he did have one problem.

He was messy.

This problem started out small. But it got bigger and bigger!

The funny thing was, René did not know he had a problem until…

…he started to lose things.

His notebook.

His favorite hat.

His book about stars.

His inkwell.

Then he found the inkwell.

Now René knew he had a problem.

"This must stop!" René said to himself.

He decided to take a walk and try to think of a solution to his problem.

It took him a moment to find his coat, his hat, and the front door.

René went to his favorite bakery to buy a fresh loaf of bread.

Then he headed to his favorite place to think: the banks of the river Seine.

René ate some of the bread while he walked. He looked at the water and wondered how he could keep better track of his things.

Night fell and René was still thinking. He was thinking so hard that he didn't look where he was going.

SPLASH!

Into the Seine went René Descartes!

When he was fished out of the water, he was cold and wet, and his bread was soggy.

René walked home. By the time he got there, he was sneezing and wheezing.

He crawled into bed and fell fast asleep.

The next morning, René still felt dreadful. Not only that, but he couldn't find a handkerchief…

or an extra blanket…

or the logs to make a fire.

He couldn't even find his soggy bread, which should have dried out by then.

René crawled sadly back into bed. He stared at his ceiling. The ceiling was the only place in his room that wasn't messy.

René wished that he lived on the neat ceiling instead of on the messy floor.

Just then, he noticed a fly on the ceiling. The fly flew off and landed near one corner.

Then it flew off and landed in another corner. Then it landed above René's toes.

Then it stopped right over René's head.

René started to think. He wondered if the fly ever landed in the same place twice. This might seem like a weird thing to think about, but René was a philosopher, so it was normal for him.

"I need to record where the fly lands so I can know how many times it lands in the same place," he thought. "But how can I do that?"

René thought and thought. Suddenly, he had a brilliant idea. It was so brilliant that he jumped out of bed and did a jig!

He knew how to record *exactly* where the fly landed on the ceiling!

René took a piece of charcoal from the fire. Then he climbed up on a chair and started drawing lines on the ceiling. (Don't try this at home—your parents won't like it.)

First René drew lines from the north wall to the south wall.

Next he drew lines from one side to the other.

Then he numbered the lines along two of the walls. After that, he got back into bed.

René watched the fly on the ceiling. When it landed, he counted the lines *over* to that spot. He wrote down the number of lines: 2.

Then he counted the lines *up* to that spot. He wrote down the number: 5.

Together, the two numbers—2 and 5—told him exactly where the fly was!

The numbers 2 and 5 are called *coordinates.* The first coordinate, 2, measures how far away the fly is from the left side. The second coordinate, 5, measures how far away the fly is from the bottom wall.

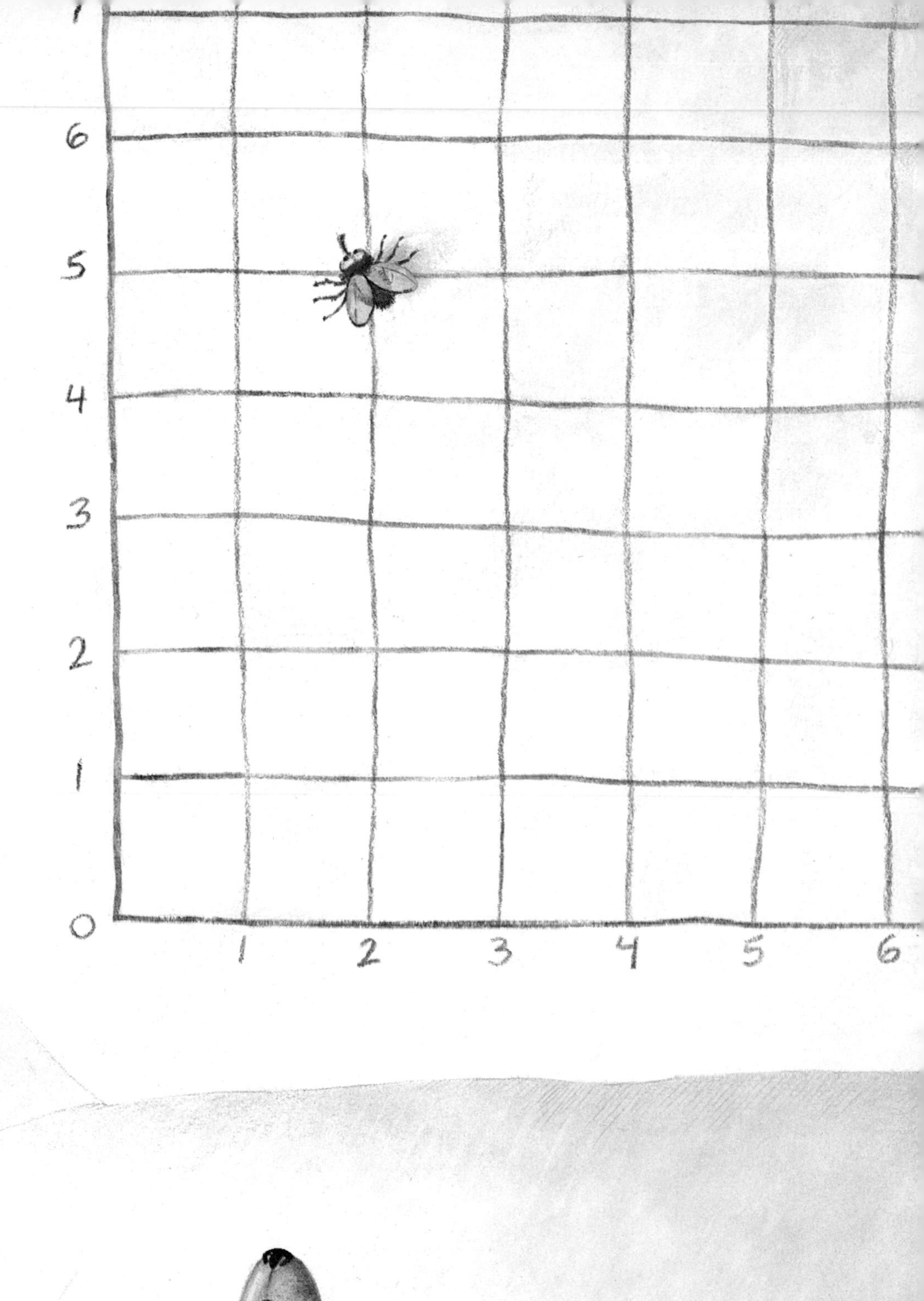
6
5
4
3
2
1
0
1
2
3
4
5
6

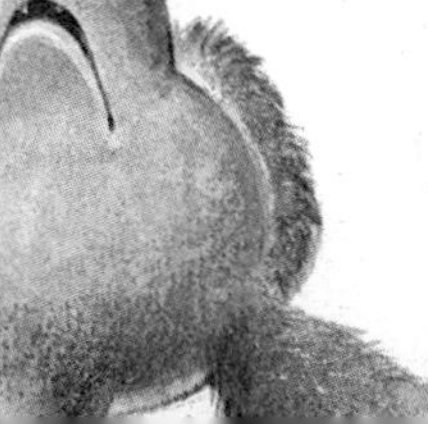

René spent the whole morning watching the fly…and sneezing.

If you had gone to visit him, he might have said, "The fly is six over, three up (6, 3)."

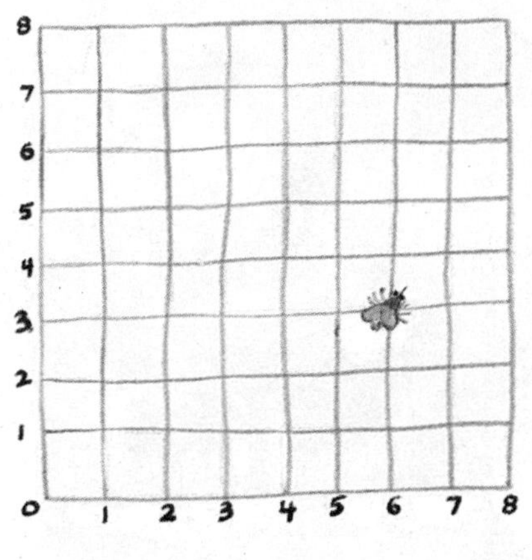

Or "The fly is four over, seven up (4, 7)."

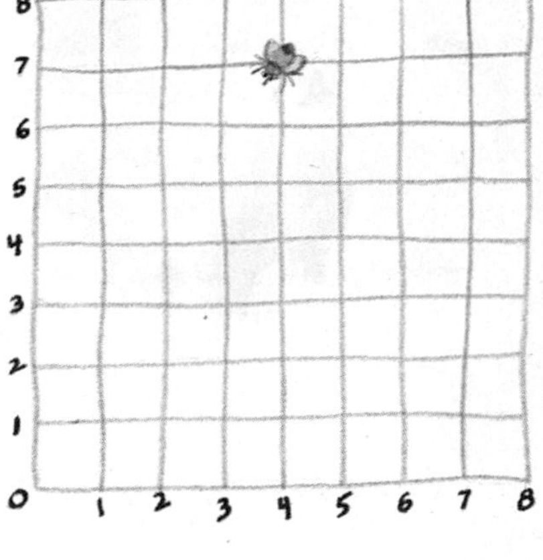

Or "The fly is eight over, one up (8, 1)."

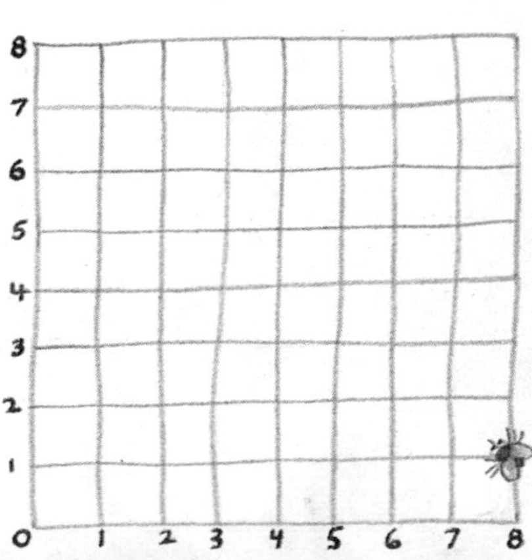

Every spot on the ceiling had its own set of coordinates!

Recording the coordinates of the fly over and over again gave René another brilliant idea.

Maybe he could keep track of his stuff the same way he kept track of the fly! It would be even easier because a hat can't get up and fly away.

René jumped out of bed again. He pushed everything into the kitchen.

Now the floor of his room was as clean as his ceiling. But he couldn't draw the grid on the floor with charcoal—it would rub off too soon.

René went next door to see if his neighbor had any paint. What luck! His neighbor was a painter!

René and the painter painted a grid on René's floor.

Then they went to the bakery to buy bread.

By the time they got back, the paint had dried. The painter helped René put his things in place on the grid.

They found René's hat, his star book, his quill pens, his old boots, his journal from when he was ten, and many other things that René didn't even know were missing.

On a chart, René carefully recorded where everything went.

Voilà!
BOOTS 4,4
STAR BOOK 4,5
CACTUS 3, 8
HAT 6,7
JOURNAL 3,
BAGEL
AEOLIPILE 6, 4
CHAMBER POT 5, 2
INK 1, 6
CANDLE
CHEESE

After that, René's home was never messy again.

Well, hardly ever.

94 95 96 97 98 99
100
75
50
25
94 95 96 97 98 99

René's system caught on around the world. It was named the *Cartesian* (car-TEE-zhen) *Coordinate System*. ("Cartesian" comes from René's last name: Des*cartes*.)

Today, people still use the Cartesian Coordinate System in many different ways.

Author's Note

Okay, so maybe René Descartes wasn't *really* messy. And maybe he didn't *really* fall into the Seine or draw lines on his ceiling.

But even if nobody knows exactly how he did it, it is a FACT that René Descartes made the Cartesian Coordinate System very popular.

And he was a darn good philosopher, too.